Super-Duper SNOWY Doodle Book

by Ryan Sias

To my hometown of Rochester, NY,
where I learned to love winter

Text and illustrations copyright © 2018 by Ryan Sias

hmhco.com

The text of this book is set in Graham.
The display type was set in Plumbsky and Eveleth Dot.

ISBN: 978-1-328-81021-2

Manufactured in China
SCP 10 9 8 7 6 5 4 3 2 1
4500720874

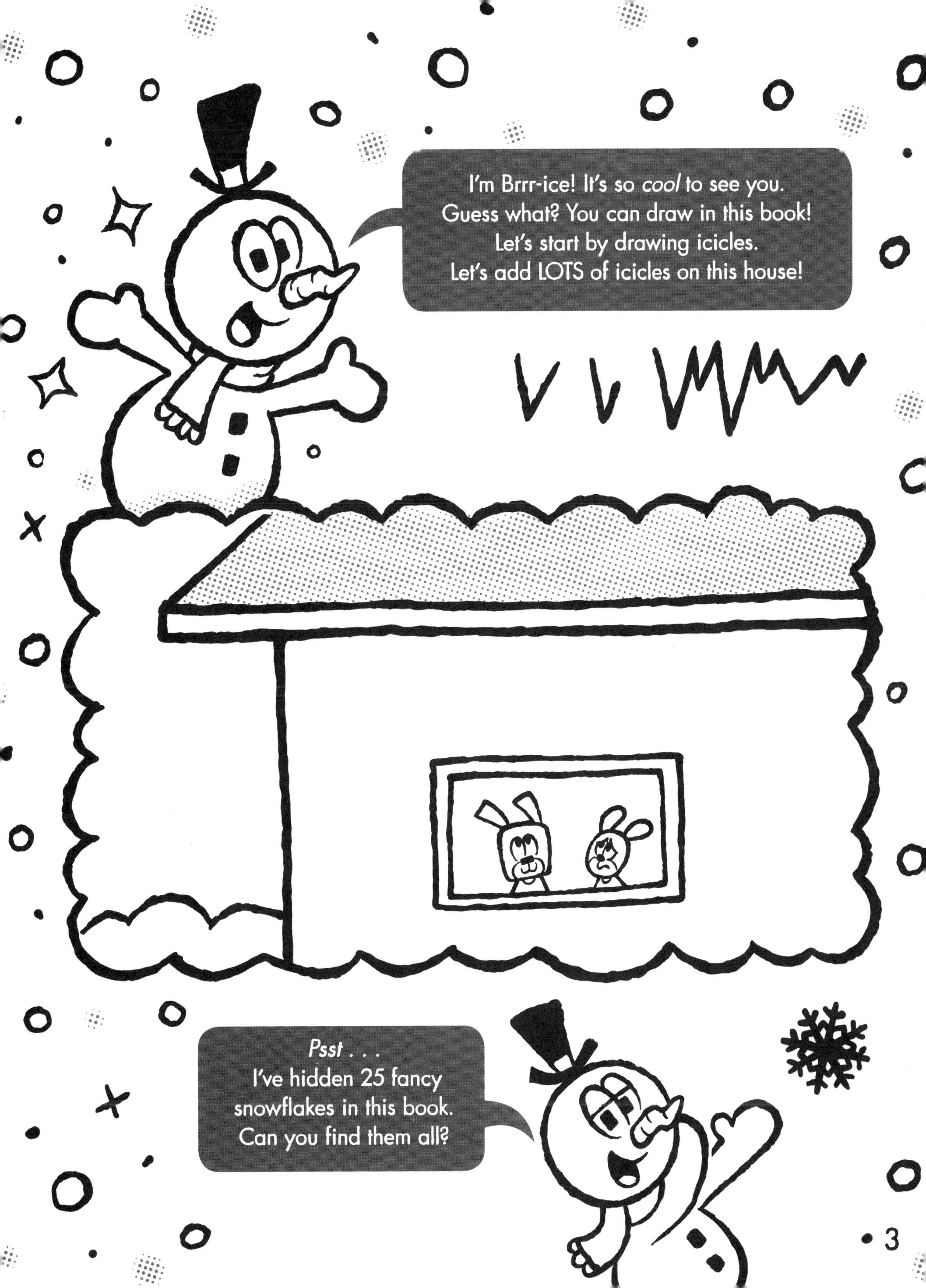
I'm Brrr-ice! It's so *cool* to see you.
Guess what? You can draw in this book!
Let's start by drawing icicles.
Let's add LOTS of icicles on this house!
Psst . . .
I've hidden 25 fancy
snowflakes in this book.
Can you find them all?

Bernie Bunny is getting ready to go out in the first snow of the year! Give Bernie a warm snowsuit.

BONUS! Give him big snow boots.

Now draw Bella Bunny a fancy jacket so she stays warm in thc chilly wind.

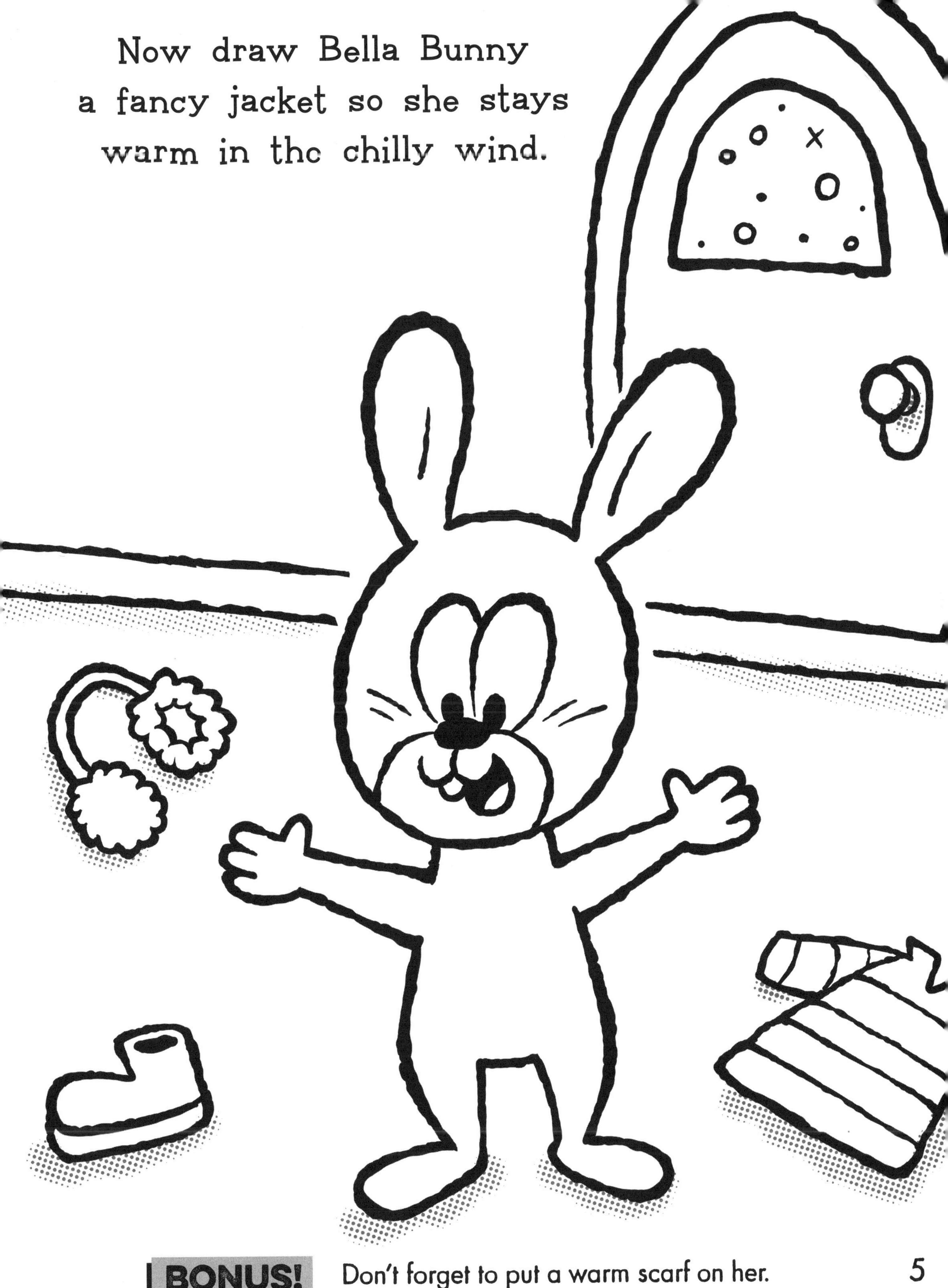

BONUS! Don't forget to put a warm scarf on her.

HOW TO DRAW

A Snowman

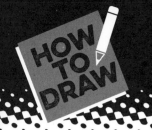

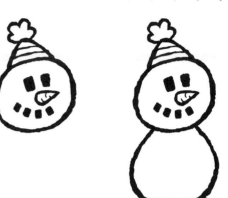

Draw your own.

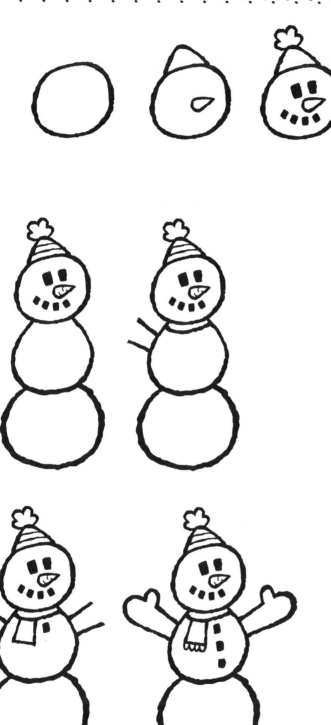

Bella and Bernie have made
a giant cool snowman—draw it!

What strange snow creatures!
Can you decorate them?

Story Starter

Bella and Bernie's snowman magically comes to life. What happens next? Write a story!

Brrr-ice takes Bella and Bernie
flying over snow-covered houses.
Draw the village below!

Jack Frost is chilling out by
freezing the pond.
Draw a frozen pond.

Make the waterfall look like ice. 11

Jack Frost flurries up
some snowflakes for Bella
and Bernie to catch
on their tongues.
Draw different snowflakes
on their tongues.

12 | **BONUS!** | Put even more snowflakes in the sky.

Find and Color the Hidden Items

pen

ice cream bar

boot

squirrel

fish

crown

canoe

igloo

moose antler

13

Shelby Squirrel

Draw your own.

14

How many squirrels can you add
to Shelby's sled?

Shelby's new sled is super fast. ✗
Draw rockets and wings on the sled.

BONUS! Give Shelby a cool helmet.

Story Starter

Oh no! Shelby is about to run into
Bella and Bernie's snowman!
What happens next? Write a story!

Daisy Deer

Draw your own.

Draw Daisy gliding on the ice
as she skates with
her friend Bernie Bunny.

Daisy got some sleek new rainbow ice skates. Color them!

BONUS! Draw blades on the ice skates.

Daisy likes to sparkle as she gracefully glides on the ice. Draw Daisy a spectacular outfit.

Daisy goes into a flurry doing lots of spins and twirls on the ice. Draw them.

BONUS! Draw Shelby Squirrel watching.

Story Starter

Baxter the Saint Bernard is spinning too fast! How does Daisy help him stop? Write a story!

Sam the Ram

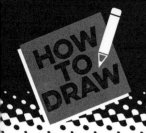

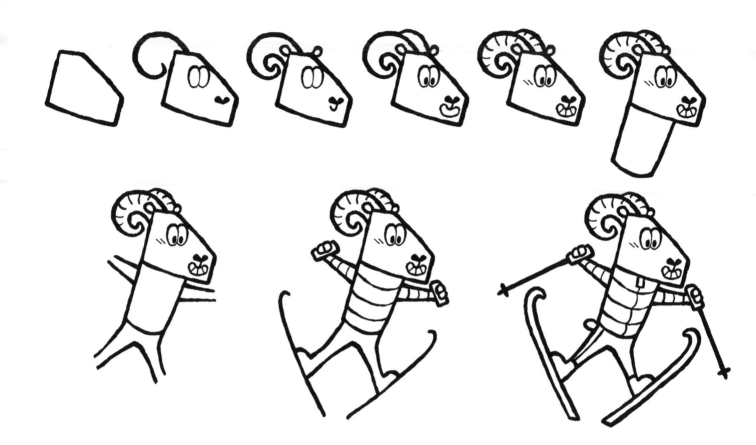

Draw your own.

Sam swoops down the ski ramp.
Draw him as he jumps off.

Oh no! Sam's tongue is
stuck to the ski lift!
Draw the expressions that
Skylar the Snow Leopard and
Brrr-ice have on their faces.

Find and Color the Hidden Items

HOW TO DRAW

Skylar the Snow Leopard

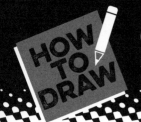

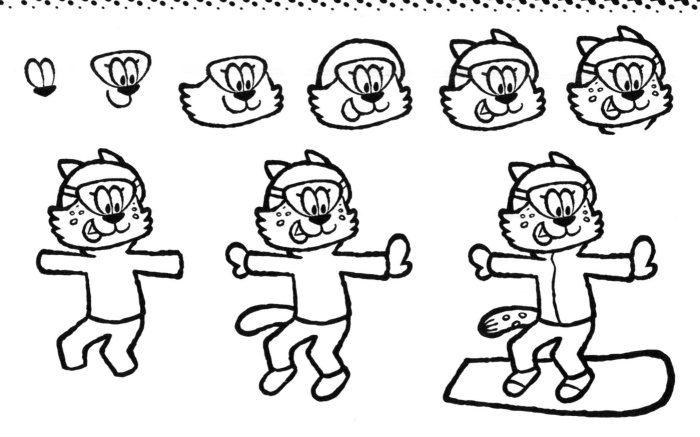

Draw your own.

Skylar is ready to grab some air
as she snowboards down the hill.
Draw her.

Skylar has a rad snowboard.
Decorate the bottom of it!

30   **BONUS!** Give Skylar cool goggles.

What is Skylar jumping over?
Draw it!

Story Starter

Oh no! Skylar finds a scared Wallace the Walrus stuck in a tree. How does she help? Write a story.

A blizzard is coming!
Time to go back to the lodge.
Fill the sky with snow.

Walcott the Wolf and Wendy the Wolf

Draw your own.

Walcott and his daughter Wendy arrive at
the ski lodge just before the blizzard hits.
Draw Walcott and Wendy coming in
with their luggage.

Walcott relaxes by the fire wearing
his favorite ugly sweater.
Draw Walcott's ugly sweater.

BONUS! Draw a fire in the fireplace.

Wendy is reading a magical book.
Draw the cover!

Walcott and Wendy are going on a moonlit ski adventure. Draw Wendy's skis and cover them with a star pattern.

BONUS! Draw twinkling stars in the sky and color it a nighttime color.

Find and Color the Hidden Items

shovel
book
cup
candy cane
carrot
sock
sled
broom
umbrella

Wallace the Walrus

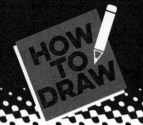

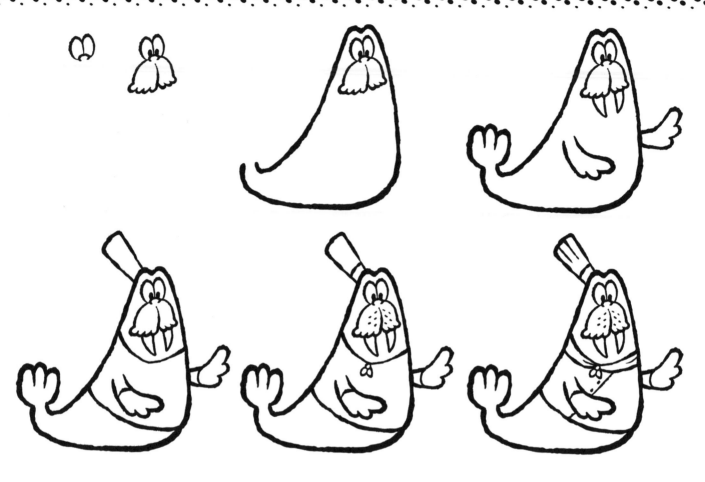

Draw your own.

Chef Wallace heats up
the kitchen with some cool creations.
Draw Chef Wallace
baking cookies.

Wallace needs help icing the cookies.
Can you decorate them?

Story Starter

One of the cookies jumps up and runs away! What happens next? Write a story!

Bruce the Moose wants to knit some soft and warm socks. Give him antlers to hold his yarn.

······· BONUS! How to Draw Antlers ·······

Bruce finished knitting the socks!
Draw what they look like.

Oh no! Caramel Cat has gotten
tangled up in the yarn!
Draw yarn all over Caramel.

Find and Color the Hidden Items

ruler
candy cane
jump rope
envelope
iceberg
sweater
scarf
broom

Becky's Plow Truck

Draw your own.

How to Draw Becky the Polar Bear

The snowplow is on the move! Draw Becky's plow truck pushing through the snow.

BONUS! Put a lot of snow in front of the plow.

49

Becky is putting spikes on her truck tires so they don't slip and slide on the road.
Draw the spikes on her tires.

Becky's truck is ready to shovel some snow! Give her truck a HUGE red snowplow!

🔍 Find and Color the Hidden Items

candle

gingerbread man

shovel

cupcake

camera

winter hat

hockey stick

crown

rabbit

lollipop

52

Baxter the Saint Bernard is snowshoeing to the lake for some wonderful wintery animal watching. What animal does Baxter see in nature?

Clark the Cardinal and Carly the Chickadee

Draw your own.

Draw your own.

54

Draw Clark and Carly nibbling some birdseed out of Baxter's hand.

Caramel Cat

Draw your own.

Caramel Cat isn't feeling too well
on this freezing cold day.
Draw Caramel in bed.

BONUS! Give Caramel a teddy bear to cuddle.

57

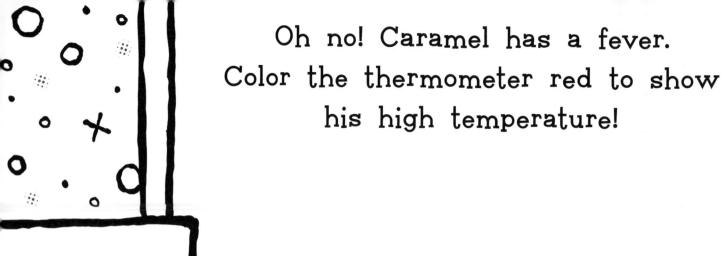

Oh no! Caramel has a fever.
Color the thermometer red to show
his high temperature!

58 **BONUS!** Put an ice pack on Caramel's hot head.

Soup will make Caramel feel better.
Add some yummy vegetables to the soup.
Don't forget to doodle noodles!

Caramel is watching
his favorite cartoon.
Draw it!

BONUS! Draw your favorite toy next to Caramel.

ice scraper

ice cream bar

mug

bell

evergreen tree

snow globe

sled

sock

snowboard

Draw your own.

Draw your own.

It's time for an icy cool slip and slide!
Draw five penguins sliding down the iceberg.

Time to get those flippers flapping! Draw a large iceberg for the penguins to dance on!

BONUS! Add more penguins dancing!

Priscilla and her friends are making
funny faces for the nature photographer.
Draw their silly faces.

Priscilla has a whale of a tale to tell! She sees a whale jumping out of the water. Draw the whale!

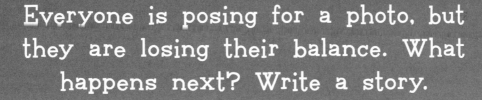

Story Starter

Everyone is posing for a photo, but they are losing their balance. What happens next? Write a story.

67

Babu the Brown Bear

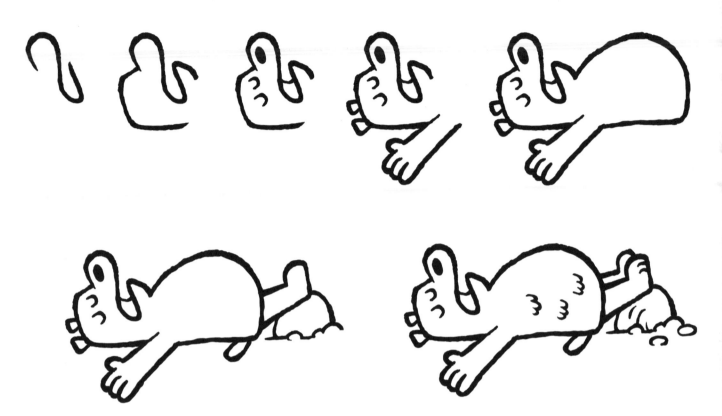

Draw your own.

Winter is Babu's time
to sleep a lot!
Draw Babu hibernating
in his cave.

BONUS! Decorate Babu's cave with lights.

Story Starter

Priscilla accidentally wakes up Babu.
What happens next?
Write a story.

ice cream cone
scarf
paintbrush
log
ski goggles
broom
pillow
glove

Paige the Puffin

Draw your own.

Paige puts on her parka and goes ice climbing. Draw Paige going up the side of the ice wall.

Paige reached the summit! Design the flag that
Paige puts on the top of the mountain.

74

Story Starter

Paige reaches the top of the mountain and finds Sapphire the Snow Princess and Yancy Yeti having hot cocoa. What happens next? Write a story.

Sapphire races to the Ice Castle.
Draw what is pulling her sleigh.

What a brrr-illiant ice castle!
Draw an ice castle for
Sapphire the Snow Princess.

Every outfit needs a little pizzazz. Draw Sapphire an icy crown and a cape with snowflakes.

BONUS! Give Sapphire the Snow Princess a staff with sparkling jewels.

seal

winter hat

bell

log

ski

glove

candle

comb

button

Yancy Yeti

Draw your own.

Yancy loves playing tricks, but not everyone realizes Yancy is a jokester. Draw Yancy scaring away a skier.

Lunchtime! With a little ice fishing,
Yancy will grab the perfect meal.
•Draw what Yancy caught for lunch.

Yancy got a cool new haircut.
Draw it.

Yancy's made a snowtastic discovery!
What kind of Ice Age animal
does Yancy find frozen in the ice?

Priscilla the Penguin is trying to get a photo of Yancy the Yeti, but she's hiding. Draw Yancy's footprints in the snow for Priscilla to follow.

BONUS! Draw Footprints

Molly the Woolly Mammoth

Draw your own.

Chill out with Molly the Woolly Mammoth.
Draw her in the Ice Age!

BONUS! Give Molly a little brother mammoth (draw a smaller woolly mammoth). What did you name him?

Simon the Saber-tooth Tiger is all smiles.
Draw his HUGE fangs!

88

Story Starter

Molly the Woolly Mammoth and Simon the Saber-tooth Tiger time travel to the future and meet Skylar, the snowboarding snow leopard. What happens next? Write a story!

It's time to prepare for
the snowball fight.
Draw lots of snowballs
in a pile.

Don't forget to build a big fort
to protect against
the flying snowballs.

Ready? Aim! Snowball!
Snowballs are thrown everywhere!
Add snowballs all over!

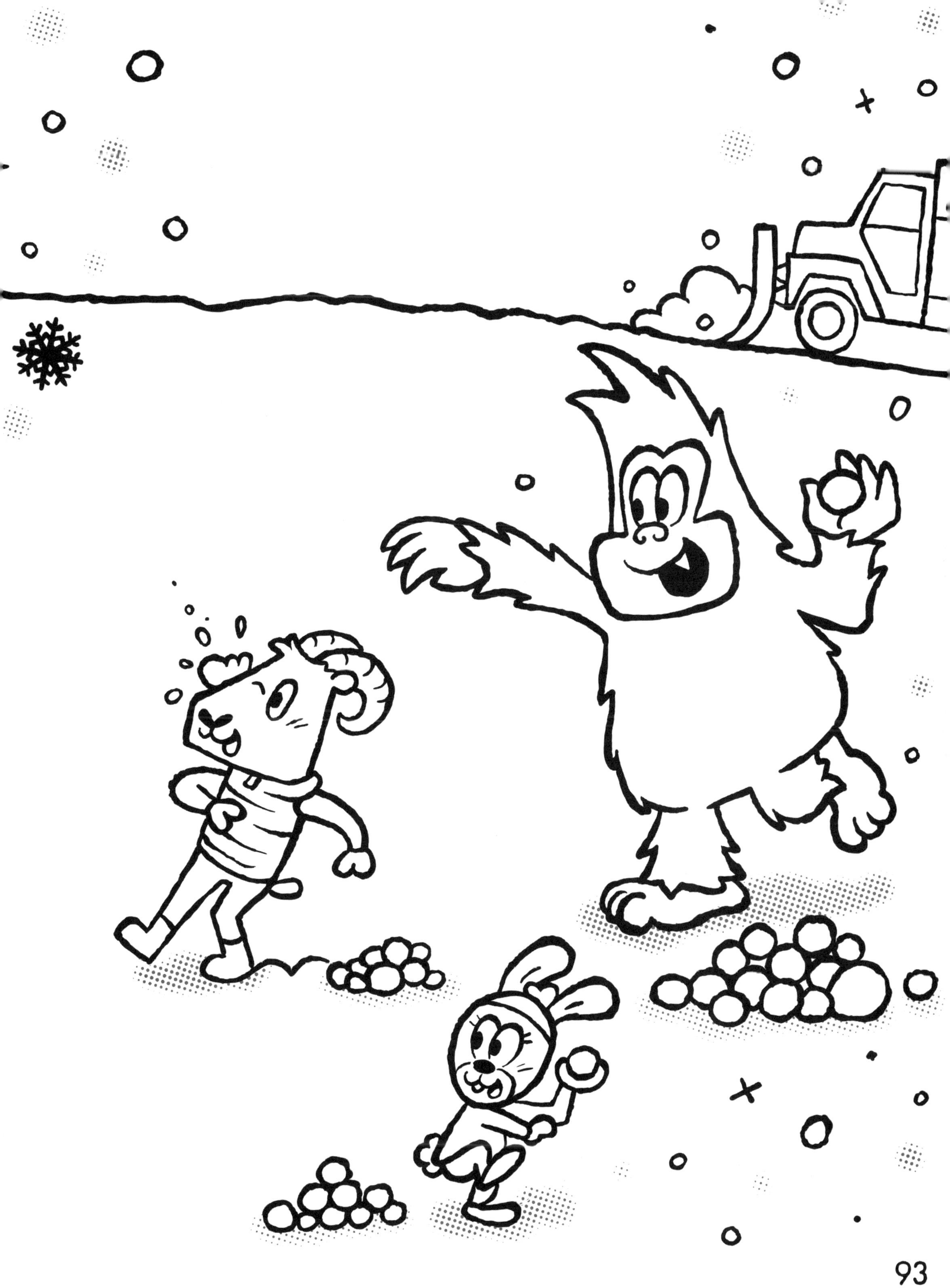

Everyone is coming inside for Wallace's
famous hot chocolate after the epic
snowball battle. Fill the cup with
hot chocolate and
marshmallows.

94 **BONUS!** Give the mug a wintry design.

It's time to celebrate a great winter with some hot chocolate and friends! Draw their mugs!

BONUS! Make the mugs different colors and sizes.

Snowtastic!

You did a cool job drawing, doodling, and writing! Did you spot all the fancy snowflakes? Color the ones you found!

Hint: Corresponding page numbers are in the center of the snowflakes.

3 7 11 12 16 19 25

27 29 31 39 42 46 50 55 64

74 76 79 82 83 87 90 92 93

p. 13

Find and Color the Hidden Items

p. 27

Find and Color the Hidden Items

p. 39

Find and Color the Hidden Items

p. 47

Find and Color the Hidden Items

p. 52

Find and Color the Hidden Items

p. 61

Find and Color the Hidden Items

p. 71

Find and Color the Hidden Items

p. 79

Find and Color the Hidden Items

Have a wonderful winter!

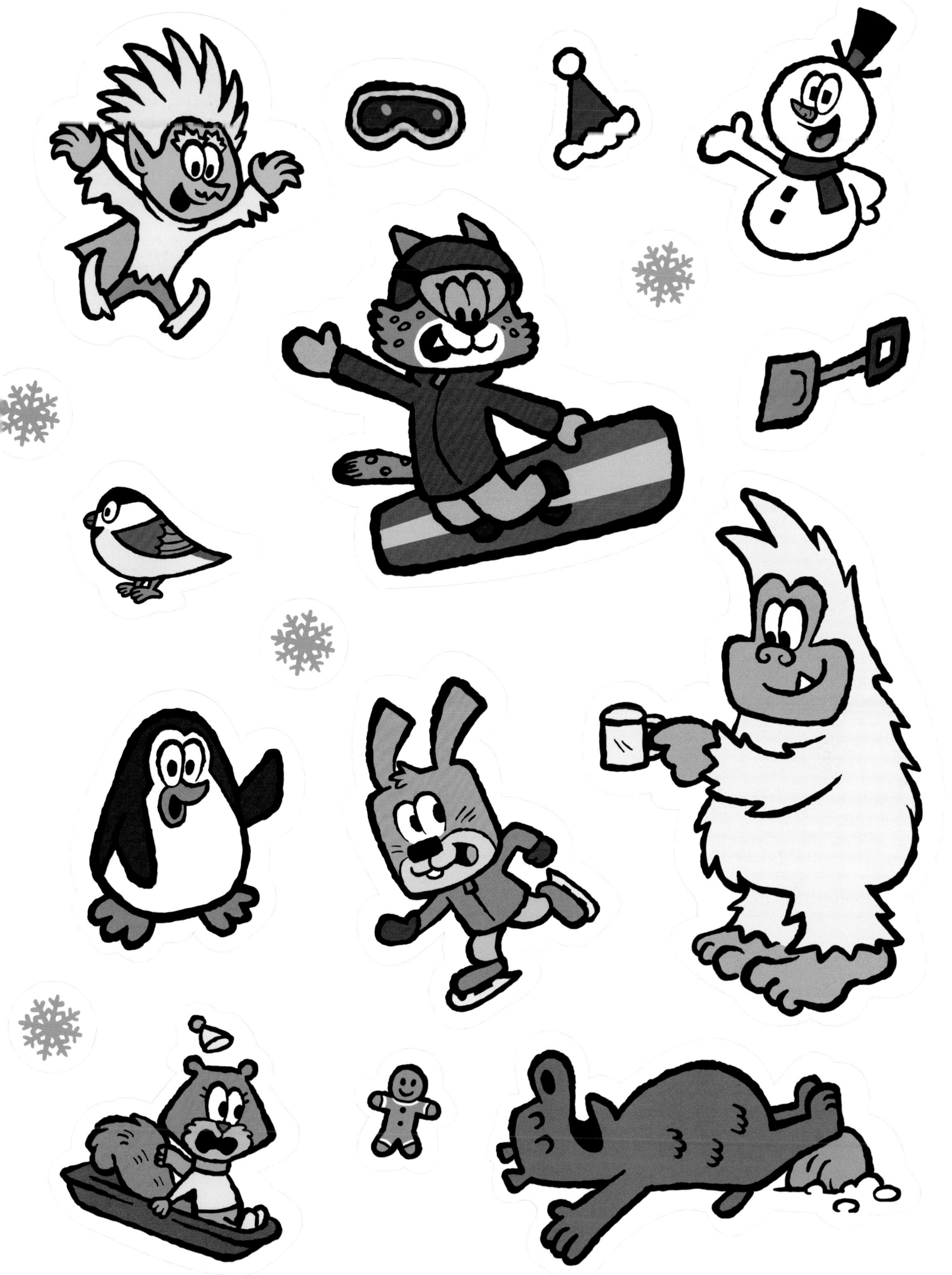

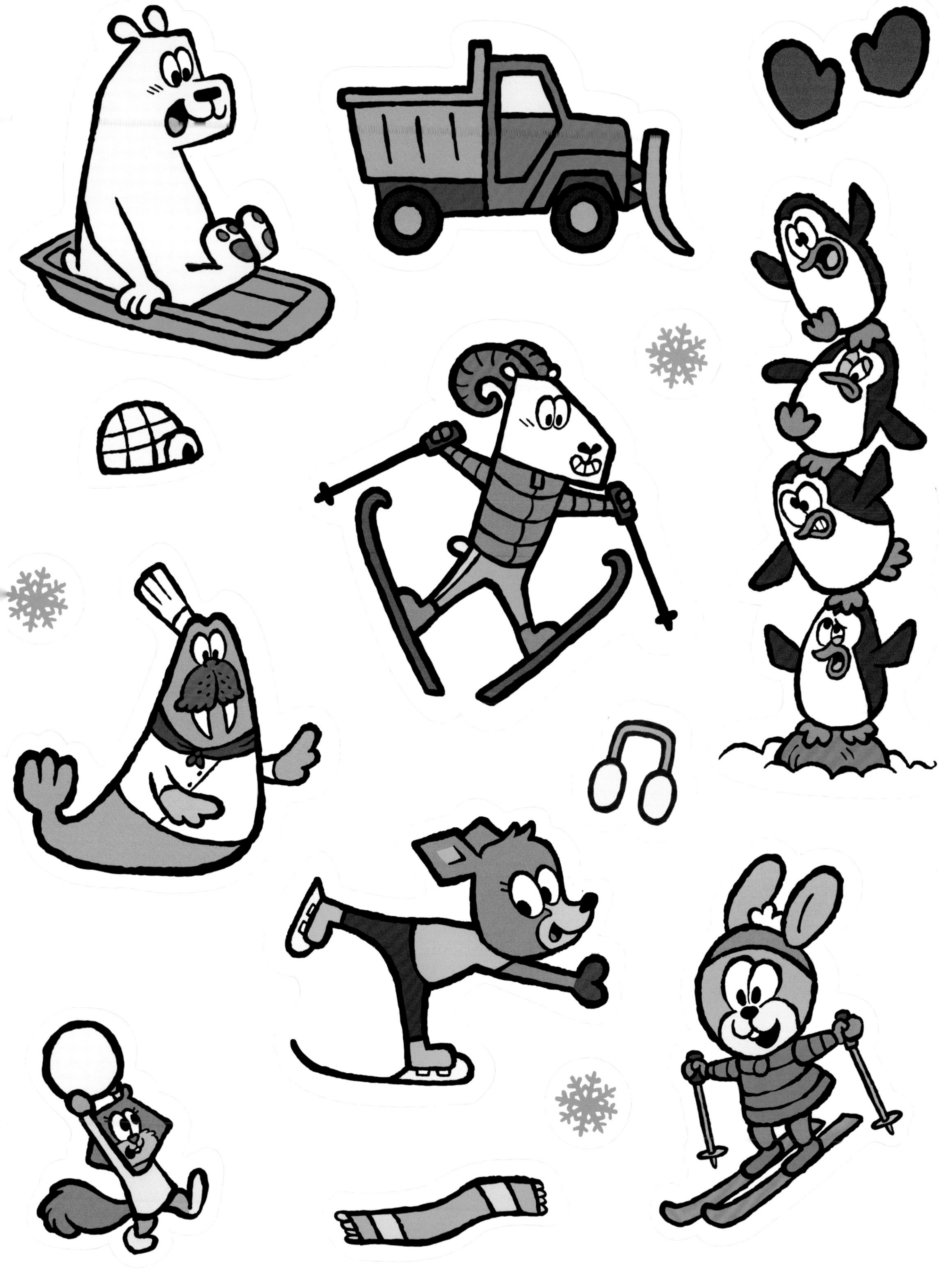

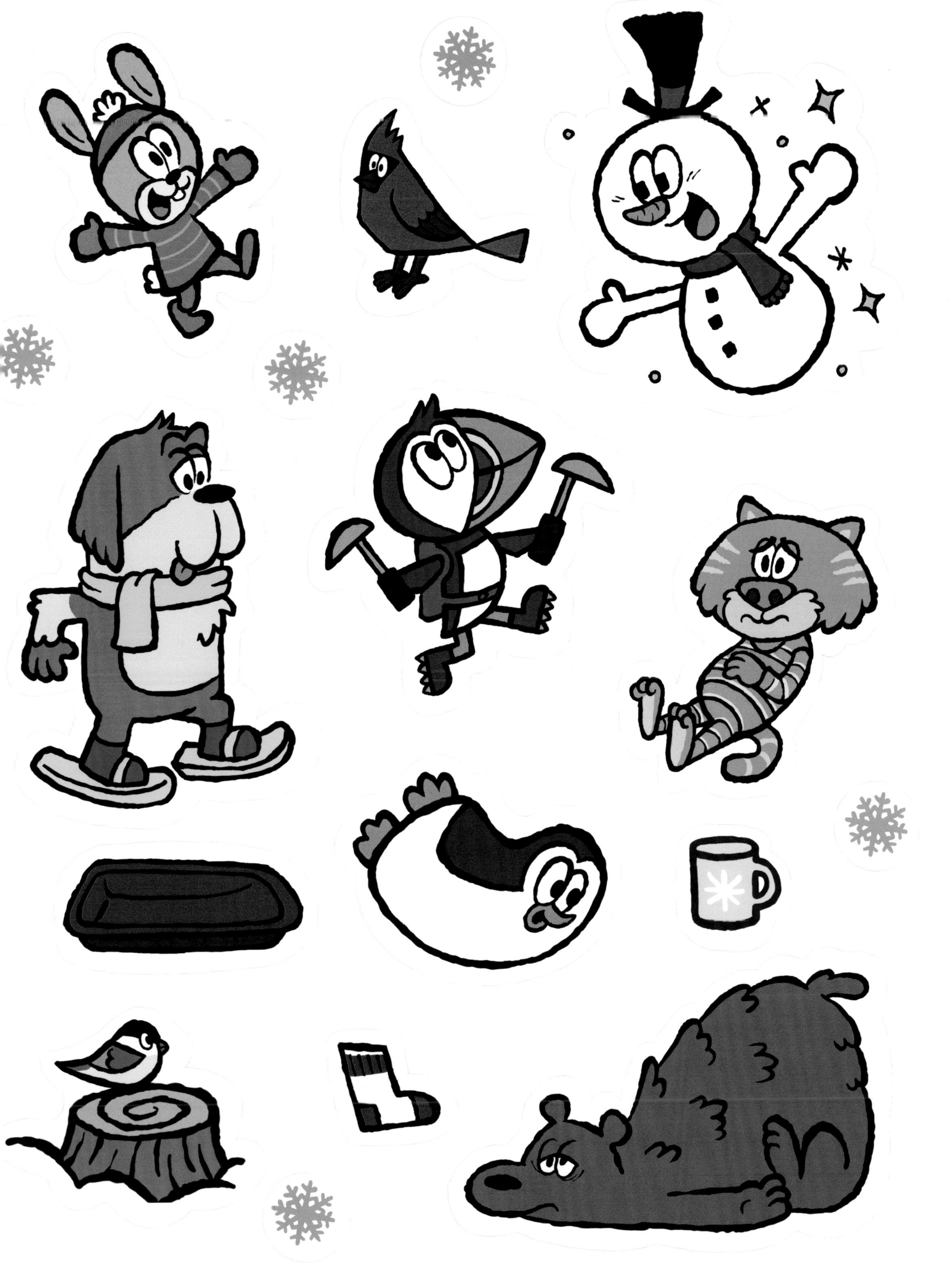

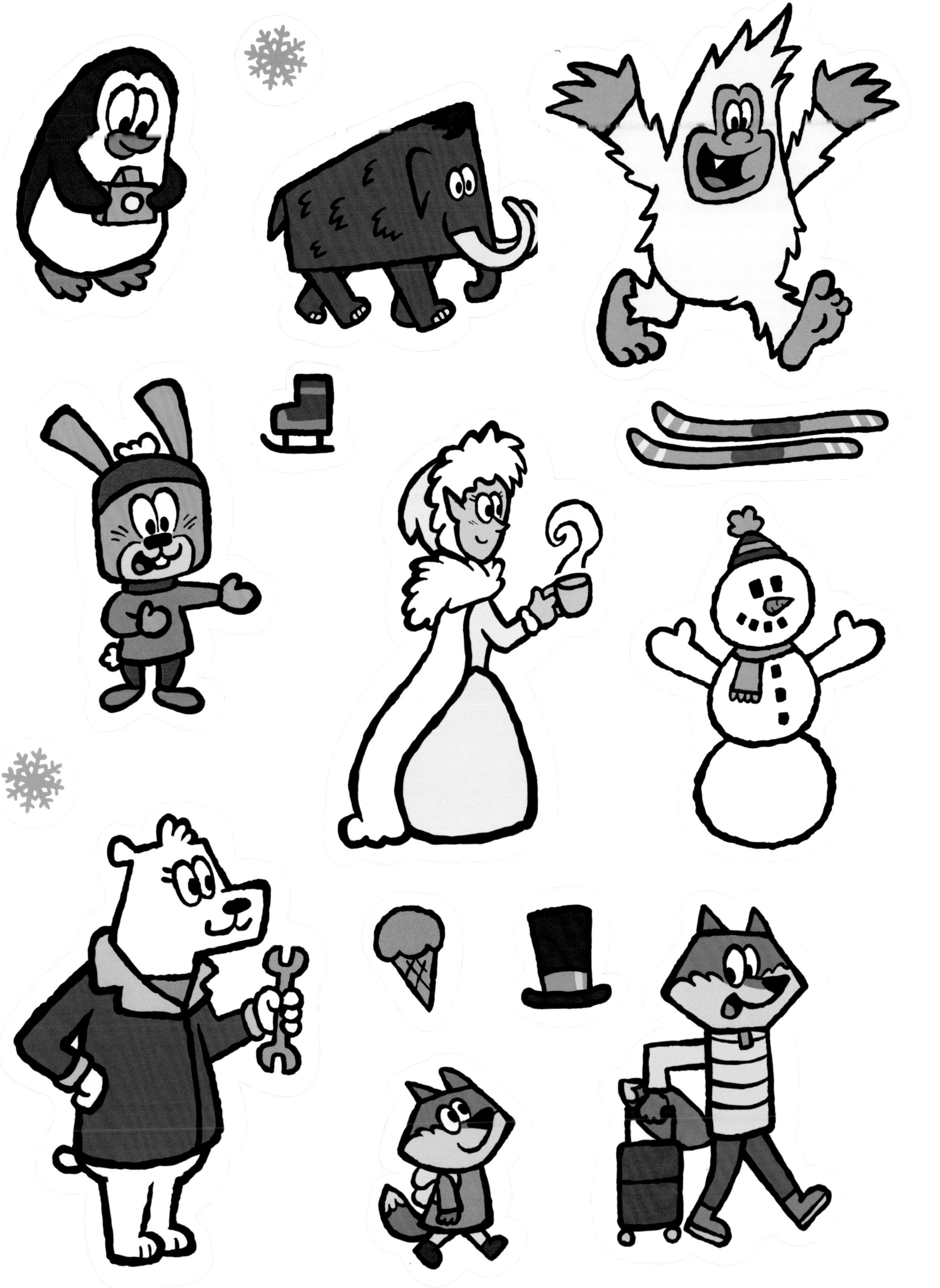